TRACY MARCHINI *illustrated by* MONIQUE FELIX

CHICKEN
Wants a Nap

Creative Editions

Text copyright © 2017 by Tracy Marchini   Illustrations copyright © 2017 by Monique Felix   Edited by Amy Novesky and Kate Riggs   Designed by Rita Marshall   Published in 2017 by Creative Editions   P.O. Box 227, Mankato, MN 56002 USA   Creative Editions is an imprint of The Creative Company   www.thecreativecompany.us   All rights reserved. No part of the contents of this book may be reproduced by any means without the written permission of the publisher.   Printed in China.   Library of Congress Cataloging-in-Publication Data   Names: Marchini, Tracy, author. / Felix, Monique, illustrator.   Title: Chicken wants a nap / by Tracy Marchini; illustrated by Monique Felix.   Summary: With the sun up and grass warm, a barnyard chicken is optimistic that it will be a comfortable day for a nap. However, forces keep conspiring against her—until it becomes a bad day for someone else. Identifiers: LCCN 2016057015 / ISBN 978-1-56846-308-7   Subjects: CYAC: 1. Chickens—Fiction. 2. Naps (Sleep)—Fiction. 3. Farm life—Fiction. BISAC: 1. JUVENILE FICTION/Animals/Farm Animals. 2. JUVENILE FICTION/Animals/Birds. 3. JUVENILE FICTION/Life-styles/Farm & Ranch Life. Classification: LCC PZ7.1.M36995 Chi 2017 / DDC [E]—dc23   First edition 9 8 7 6 5 4 3 2 1

IT'S A GOOD DAY TO BE A CHICKEN. THE SUN IS UP.

The grass is warm. And Chicken wants a nap.

BACAWK!

It's a bad day to be a chicken. The rain is falling.

Her feathers are wet. Chicken cannot nap.

It's a good day to be a chicken.

The barn is quiet.

The nest is dry.

And Chicken wants a nap.

MOO!

IT'S A BAD DAY TO BE A CHICKEN.

THE COWS ARE LOUD.

The barn is smelly. Chicken cannot nap.

It's a good day to be a chicken. The farmer is kind.

THE PORCH IS COVERED. AND CHICKEN WANTS A NAP.

WOOF!

IT'S A BAD DAY TO BE A CHICKEN.

THE DOG IS TOO FRIENDLY. THE PORCH IS TOO SMALL.

Chicken cannot nap.

IT'S A GOOD DAY TO BE A CHICKEN.

THE RAIN HAS STOPPED. THE WORMS ARE OUT.

HER BELLY IS FULL.

And Chicken naps.

IT'S A BAD DAY TO BE A WORM.